The Rocket Ship Bed Trip

N. Jane Quackenbush
Illustrations by Lynne Villalobos

Hidden Wolf Books
St. Augustine, Florida

Tonight my bed

Took off from my room.

It raced through the sky,

Heading straight for the moon!

Up, around,
And beyond the stars,

Past Venus, Mercury,
And back to Mars!

I look about
And hold on tight
As we zig to the left
And zag to the right.

Gravity is gone,
My bunny floats out.
"Where are you going?"
I begin to shout.

Floating deep
Into the night,

Together we orbit
Like a satellite.

From way up here,
Earth seems so small—
Or could it be
That I'm this tall?

Meteors and asteroids
Dart and dash.

I twist and turn
To avoid a crash!

Nebulae here,
Exploding stars there.

I see space junk. …
Look—there goes a chair!

The galaxies swirl;
Their many stars glow.

I gaze and wonder:
Where do they all go?

The stars are bright as any day.
I must be in the Milky Way!

This makes me think of
Candies and caramel,
So I take a whiff
And begin to smell …

Morning coffee
And breakfast tea;
The whistling kettle
awakens me.

I open my eyes
And see the sun.
My dream is over …
The day has begun!

Saturn

These photos of space were taken with the help of a telescope. Can you find the celestial bodies pictured here within the story? Can you find more?

What do you see in the night sky from *your* room?

The Horsehead Nebula

The Moon

Comet

Jupiter

The Whirlpool Galaxy

For more space photos, information about rocket ships, or to join the NASA Kids' Club, go to NASA.gov.

For my children, Christian and Westly.
N. Jane Quackenbush

For Kai and his "Bunbun."
Lynne Villalobos

Publisher's Cataloging-In-Publication

Quackenbush, N. Jane.
  The rocket ship bed trip / N. Jane Quackenbush ; illustrations by
Lynne Villalobos. -- 1st ed.
    p. : ill. ; cm.

  Summary: In this rhyming story, a child's bed turns into a rocket
ship and travels through outer space. He encounters planets, stars,
galaxies, comets, and asteroids before returning to his bedroom,
where he awakens to sunshine and the smell of breakfast.
  Interest age level: 003-008.
  Issued also as an ebook.
  ISBN: 978-0-9911045-0-5

  1. Space flight--Juvenile fiction. 2. Space ships--Juvenile fiction.
3. Astronomy--Juvenile fiction. 4. Beds--Juvenile fiction. 5. Space
flight--Fiction. 6. Space ships--Fiction. 7. Astronomy--Fiction. 8.
Beds--Fiction. 9. Stories in rhyme. I. Villalobos, Lynne. II. Title.

PZ7.Q335 Ro 2014
[E]

Printed and bound in USA
First Edition 2014

CPSIA information can be obtained
at www.ICGtesting.com
Printed in the USA
BVHW060033031019
560016BV00009B/153/P